GOES ON HOLIDAY

Inside the dome there was an enormous main swamp, with smaller swamps around it. We saw a machine which made giant bubbles rise out of the mud. You could sit on them until they popped. There were also lots of slides.

They were pretty amazing, too. One was enormous. It was called The Big Whizzer, and it had so many twists and turns I thought you'd probably get dizzy coming down it.

TONY BRADMAN

DiLLY

GOES ON HOLIDAY

Illustrated by Susan Hellard

mammoth

First published in Great Britain1990
by Piccadilly Press Ltd
Published 1992 by Mammoth
an imprint of Egmont Children's Books Ltd
Michelin House, 81 Fulham Road, London SW3 6RB

Reprinted 1992 (three times)
Reissued 1993
Reprinted 1993, 1994 (three times), 1995 (twice), 1996, 1997,1998

Text copyright © Tony Bradman, 1990
Illustrations copyright © Susan Hellard, 1990

The right of Tony Bradman to be identified as author
of this work and of Susan Hellard to be identified as
the illustrator has been asserted by them in accordance
with the Copyright, Designs and Patents Act 1988

ISBN 0 7497 0433 0

A CIP catalogue record for this title
is available from the British Library

Printed and bound in Great Britain
by Cox & Wyman Ltd, Reading, Berkshire

Contents

DILLY AND THE SPORTS DAY

"Mother," said my little brother Dilly at breakfast this morning,
"I don't feel very well."

Mother felt his forehead. He didn't have a temperature, so she asked him if he had a pain. Dilly nodded.

"Where does it hurt?" said Mother.

"Here," said Dilly. He pointed to his stomach. "And here, and here, and here, and here . . ." he said, pointing to his head, his tail, and lots of places in between.

1

Mother looked up and winked at Father over Dilly's head.

"I see," she said with a smile. "This doesn't have anything to do with it being your school Sports Day today, does it?"

"No, Mother," said Dilly. "Of *course* not."

Dilly had got very excited about Sports Day last year. He'd been sure he was

going to win all his races. But he hadn't, and he'd been very disappointed and sulky for weeks afterwards.

So I wasn't surprised when he said he didn't want to be in Sports Day this year.

He had tried very hard to get out of it, too. He told Mother and Father there wasn't going to be a Sports Day. He even hid the letter from school which said when it was. Mother had found it screwed up at the bottom of his book bag.

Now he was pretending to be ill so he could stay at home.

"You look fine to me, Dilly," said Mother. "In fact, judging by the way you were misbehaving in the bathroom this morning, I don't think there's much wrong with you at all."

"Well, I'm *not* going to school," said Dilly crossly. "And I won't be in stupid old Sports Day, either, so there!"

He pushed away his bowl of fern flakes. It bumped into his glass of pineapple juice and knocked it over. A big puddle of juice spread across the table.

Mother looked cross, and I think Dilly realised he was about to get told off. So he quickly said he was sorry, then jumped down from his chair and ran to get a cloth.

"I'll wipe up the mess, Mother," he said, with his I-Know-I've-Been-Naughty-But-I'll-Try-To-Be-Better smile. "And I'll be good from now on, I promise."

"Don't think you can get round me that way, Dilly," said Mother, taking the cloth. "I know you too well. You're going to school, and that's that."

Dilly's smile disappeared, and was replaced with a scowl.

"Come on, Dilly," said Father. "It won't be that bad. Tell him how much he'll enjoy it, Dorla."

I did. I told Dilly how exciting Sports Day was at my school. I could hardly wait for it to come round every year.

"But Dorla always wins something," said Dilly. It was true, I usually did win at least one race. "I bet I come last every time. I'm no good at *anything*."

"Yes you are, Dilly," said Father. He smiled and put his arm round Dilly's shoulders. "And you shouldn't worry about coming first or last, anyway. Being with your friends and taking part is what *really* matters."

Mother and Father talked to him for a while longer, but he didn't look convinced. So there are no prizes for guessing what he did when Father said it was time to go to school.

That's right ... Dilly opened his mouth and fired off an ultra-special, 150-mile-per-hour super-scream, the kind that's *so* loud it makes your ears ring and your teeth ache.

In the end, Father had to carry him out of the door under his arm.

"'Bye, Dilly!" said Mother. There was no reply, although Dilly's tail did twitch once or twice.

Mother and Father had arranged to have the afternoon off work so they could be there to cheer Dilly on. As most of my friends had little brothers or sisters at Dilly's school, we had been given the afternoon off as well.

The morning went by very quickly. Mother and Father picked me up after lunch, and we headed for Dilly's school. It was a sunny day. Mother said that at least we knew the weather would be good, even if Dilly wasn't. Father and I laughed.

By the time we arrived, the sports field behind the school was already crowded with families, most of whom we knew. Some of them were having picnics, and there were plenty of grown-ups chasing excited dinosaur toddlers.

A racing track had been marked out in white lines on the grass. Beyond it I could see Dilly and his classmates. Mother, Father and I waved, but Dilly didn't wave back. He was still looking very sulky.

"Quieten down everybody, please," I heard someone saying. It was Mrs Dactyl, Dilly's teacher. She looked rather hot and flustered. "I'd like you all to listen while I go through a few things. And you can't listen if you're pulling Durna's tail, can you now, Darryl?"

Mrs Dactyl explained that this year they would be divided into four teams – red, blue, yellow and orange. So even if they didn't win a race themselves, they still had a chance of being in a winning team.

"Right," she said at last, "I want you to line up quietly while Mrs Deemi hands out the sashes. Then we can get started ... and may the best team win!"

Dilly, I noticed, was in the orange team. He wouldn't put his sash on at first, but he did after Mrs Dactyl said something to him. Then I lost sight of him when the runners lined up for the first race. Dilly wasn't one of them.

The nicest thing about Sports Day for dinosaurs of Dilly's age is that there are lots of funny events. At my Sports Day we don't have sack races, or egg and spoon races.

I liked the train race best. That's the one where you have to keep stopping to put on some clothes, then pick up a hat, a suitcase and an umbrella. So you don't have to be a fast runner to win it, just good at getting dressed quickly.

Dilly wasn't in it. We weren't surprised about that. Father said the only thing

Dilly knows to do with clothes is to get them dirty. He's certainly never been very good at putting them on.

But when he didn't appear in the next race, or the race after that, Mother and Father began to look a little worried.

"I think we'd better have a word with Mrs Dactyl," said Father after a while.

It turned out Dilly was refusing to go in *any* of the races. He was sitting on his tail with his back to the track.

"I won't make him go in a race if he doesn't want to," said Mrs Dactyl. Then she smiled. "I do have an idea, though . . . and knowing Dilly, it *might* just work."

She wouldn't tell us what she had in mind. But we didn't have to wait long to find out.

"Can I have your attention, everybody?" she called out a moment later. Dilly didn't move. "I haven't heard much cheering so far. Now in the next race, I want to hear you all rooting for your teams as *loudly* as you can! In fact, I'll give a special prize to the dinosaur with the loudest cheer."

Dilly turned round. And for the first time that day, he didn't look at all sulky . . .

Of course, Dilly won the prize for the loudest cheer by miles. He practically deafened everybody. And you should have seen his face when Mrs Dactyl pinned a special gold badge onto his sash. I've never seen such a big smile.

After that there was no stopping him. He went in for every race he could, and he did very well.

Best of all, he and his friend Darryl won the two-tails race. You know what that is – it's when the two of you run with your tails tied together.

Mrs Dactyl came over to congratulate him. Then she asked Father if he was going in for the parents' race. Father laughed and said he didn't think so, as he wasn't a very good runner, and would probably come last.

"You shouldn't worry about coming first or last, Father," said Dilly with a cheeky smile. He even sounded a little like Father as he said it. "Being with your friends and taking part is what *really* matters."

"Dilly," said Father, who was smiling too, "what would we do without you?"

I opened my mouth ... but I didn't say a word.

DILLY AND THE MAGIC SHOW

A little while ago, Dilly and I watched a new programme on TV. It was called *The Dinosaur Magic Show*, and the star was a terrific magician called The Great Bronto.

Dilly could hardly believe his eyes, especially when The Great Bronto made his helper vanish in a puff of smoke.

"Oh, wow!" he said. "Is it *really* magic, Mother?"

"I don't think so, Dilly," said Mother.

She explained that magicians used special tricks to make what they did *look* like magic. She said the helper had probably slipped away without anyone seeing. Dilly looked thoughtful.

"Do you think *I* could learn to do magic, Mother?" he said.

"I don't see why not," said Mother. "We could go to the library and look for a book about it, if you like."

We found just the right book, too – *The Young Dinosaur's Guide to Magic,* by The Great Bronto himself. And from the moment Mother read it to him, it was all Dilly talked about.

Mother and Father said they were glad he was doing something he enjoyed. They gave him an old hat to pull things out of, and a pack of cards to do tricks with. But I soon got fed up with it. Dilly was a real pest.

He was always following me round saying things like, "Pick a card, Dorla, any card," and "Hocus, pocus, diplodocus." He got cross if I wouldn't play with him. But I didn't want to, mostly because his tricks never worked. That made him cross, too.

A couple of days later, Dilly's best

friend Dixie came round to play. You can probably guess what game Dilly suggested.

"Let's play magic, Dixie!" he said, before she'd even got in the door. "I'll be The Great Bronto, and you can be my helper."

Dixie didn't seem sure at first, but it wasn't long before she stopped being Dilly's helper, and was pretending to be a great magician herself.

"Well, you two have been very good today," said Mother when we all sat down at the table. Dixie was staying for supper. "That's a game you should definitely play more often."

"It isn't a *game*, Mother," said Dilly in between mouthfuls of toasted swamp worms. "We're *real* magicians."

"I beg your pardon, Dilly," laughed Mother. "Does that mean you'll be doing a show on TV?"

"No," said Dixie, before Dilly could say anything. "But we could put on a show for all our friends."

"What a good idea!" said Father. "Though why don't you make it a *neighbourhood* magic show? That would be *much* more fun!"

Dilly obviously thought so too. He'd just taken a huge slurp of pineapple juice, and got so excited he nearly choked.

Once he'd recovered, we decided the show would be in the garden on Saturday, and that we would invite family, friends and neighbours. Father said he would help Dilly put together a proper magician's costume. Dilly said he couldn't wait.

First we made some invitations. I did the writing, and Dilly and Dixie drew the pictures. Mother got them copied at work, and we handed them out in the neighbourhood and at Dilly's school. This is what they said:

GRAND MAGIC SHOW AT THE
DINOSAUR HOUSE!
Two o'clock Saturday afternoon – bring your friends and see Dynamic Dixie and . . . The Fabulous Dilly!
(Entry free)

As soon as she found out about it, my friend Deena wanted to help. Mother said our job could be to introduce the show. We asked if we could also do a dance we had learned at ballet class. Mother said that would be lovely.

Father worked hard on Dilly's costume. He made him a top hat out of cardboard painted black, a big, flowing cape from some material Mother had, and a magic wand that was just like The Great Bronto's.

"You look terrific, Dilly," said Mother. "Now all you've got to do is concentrate on getting your tricks right."

That was the problem. No matter how hard he tried, Dilly couldn't make his tricks come out quite as well as Dixie's. Dilly didn't say anything, but I knew he didn't like the fact that Dixie was better at magic than him.

"Never mind, Dilly," said Mother. "You'll just have to keep trying. I'm sure it will be all right on the day."

Dilly didn't look so sure.

On Saturday morning, Mother draped some curtains over one of the giant fern's branches to make a stage. We hung up balloons, and some tinsel from Christmas. Then we put out chairs for the audience. It looked very impressive.

Soon everyone started to arrive. Grandma and Grandpa came with Aunt Dimpla and baby Deevoo. Dixie's parents turned up next, and then some of Dilly's friends from school, followed by most of our neighbours.

The last one to come was Mr Doon, a very, very old dinosaur who lived just along the road. I showed him to a seat at the front, and said I hoped he would enjoy the show.

"What's that, my dear?" he said,
tapping a small plastic thing in one of
his ears. "You'll have to speak more
loudly, I'm afraid. My hearing aid is
playing up today."

But I didn't have time to talk. We had
to start the show.

Deena and I stepped out in front of

the curtains and welcomed everyone to
The Grand Magic Show. Then we
introduced the first act. It was us doing
our dance. I was very nervous, but it
went well, if the applause was anything
to go by.

Next it was Dixie's turn, and she was
very good. She did a terrific card trick,

made some coins disappear and, finally, produced lots and lots of paper flowers from one of her pockets. She got plenty of applause, too.

"And now," I said after Dixie had left the stage, "the act you've all been waiting for – the amazing, the incredible, the fabulous . . . DILLY!"

Things didn't go too badly at first. Dilly started with a card trick he'd almost got right once or twice.

But the card he was supposed to find by magic fell out of his sleeve, and somebody giggled. Dilly hurried on to his next trick.

That went wrong too, as did the next one, *and* the next one. I could see Dilly was upset.

For his last trick, Dilly put a coin under one of three cups on a small table. He moved them around, and the audience had to guess where the coin was. Only Dilly was supposed to know.

But when he lifted the cup he thought it was under, there was no coin. He lifted another cup, but that was the wrong one too. Dilly's bottom lip started to quiver. Then someone called out, "Try the middle one!" and everybody laughed.

That's when I held my breath, because I had a pretty good idea of what was coming. Dilly opened his mouth . . . and blasted off an ultra-special, 150-mile-per-hour super-scream, the kind that makes the small cups you use for magic tricks explode into tiny little pieces.

I thought the whole audience would dive for cover, and nearly everyone did. But when Dilly quietened down and I surfaced, I saw Mr Doon still sitting there, clapping. He stopped once to tap his hearing aid, then started clapping again, even harder.

"Bravo!" he called out. "What a terrific trick!"

Suddenly I realised what had

happened. Mr Doon's hearing aid wasn't working, so he hadn't heard Dilly's scream. He thought the cups exploding had all been part of the trick!

Gradually the others started to laugh and clap too, and soon Dilly was smiling.

Deena and I hurried on to announce the show was over, and we all took a final bow. Then Mother brought out some fern cakes and swamp juice. Everybody stayed until quite late.

And the next day, Dilly asked Mother if we could put on another Grand Magic Show as soon as possible.

"I know how to do really good tricks now," he said. "I just have to scream."

"The only way we'll all come," said Mother sternly, "is if everyone gets a hearing aid like Mr Doon's."

Then Mother winked and gave him a hug.

DILLY GOES ON HOLIDAY

"Everybody ready?" said Father, turning
on the dino-car's engine. "OK then ...
Swamp Land, here we come!"

We were going to Swamp Land on
holiday, and Dilly and I were very excited
about it. In fact, Dilly hadn't talked
about anything else for weeks.

"Now, Dilly," said Mother once we
were on our way. "I hope you haven't
forgotten what I told you last night."

"What was that, Mother?" asked Dilly.

He looked puzzled.

"Dilly Dinosaur," sighed Mother, "I sometimes wonder if you listen to a single word I say. I said you were to remember this holiday was for *all* of us, and not just for you. You'll have plenty of fun, but your father and I need a rest, too."

Dilly was looking even more puzzled now.

"But why do you need a rest, Mother?" he said. "You sleep a lot anyway. It took me *ages* to wake you up this morning."

It was true. Dilly had got up very early and run into Mother and Father's bedroom. They had been quite cross.

"Because we're tired, Dilly," said Mother. "We've both got jobs, there's the housework to do, Dorla and you to look after ... This holiday is our only chance to relax."

"And we don't want you to spoil it," said Father. "Which is why we're going to Swamp Land. As soon as we heard about The Tiny Tails, we knew it was the place for us."

Mother and Father had already told us about The Tiny Tails. It's a Swamp Land club run by specially trained leaders. They keep young dinosaurs like us entertained while our parents enjoy themselves and get some rest.

I said I thought it would be fun.

"I'm sure you're right, Dorla," said Mother. "You think so too, don't you, Dilly?"

"Yes, Mother," said Dilly. But he didn't sound very sure. And from the look on his face I could tell he didn't understand.

Mother and Father didn't notice, though.

It was a long journey to Swamp Land, so it was almost dark when we arrived. We picked up the key to our villa at an office with a sign that said 'Reception'.

"Are we going to start having fun now?" asked Dilly as soon as we had unloaded our suitcases from the dino-car.

"Not just yet, Dilly," laughed Mother. "It's late, and we're all tired. The fun will begin tomorrow, though, I promise."

Dilly went to bed without any more argument. But I had a feeling he would be getting up pretty early the next day too ...

I was right. He ran into Mother and Father's room while they were still asleep and jumped on top of them.

"It's tomorrow, Mother!" he shouted. "So it's time to have fun. Yippee!"

Mother groaned. She tried to pull the covers over her head, but Father wouldn't let her.

"Let's give her the tickle treatment," said Father. "That ought to get her up, the lazybones!"

Dilly and I laughed, and started tickling Mother. Soon she was laughing too. She didn't stay in bed very much longer. We had breakfast, then went to have a look round.

In the centre of Swamp Land there

was a huge glass dome. As we walked towards it, we went past shops, a sports hall, playgrounds, a beauty parlour, basking rooms and places where you could eat, including a McDinosaur's.

Inside the dome there was an enormous main swamp, with smaller swamps around it. We saw a machine which made giant bubbles rise out of the mud. You could sit on them until they popped. There were also lots of slides.

They were pretty amazing, too. One was enormous. It was called The Big Whizzer, and it had so many twists and turns I thought you'd probably get dizzy coming down it.

"Wow, Dilly, look at that!" said Father as someone came flying out of the end. "I'll bet you can't wait to have a go!"

Dilly looked ... but he didn't say anything.

I was keen to get changed and start wallowing, but Mother said we had something else to do first. She wanted to get Dilly and me signed up for The Tiny Tails.

"Hi there!" said a large dinosaur at The Tiny Tails' office. "My name's Dinsdale, and I'm *really* glad to meet you!"

He had a loud, booming voice, and lots of shiny white teeth which he showed when he smiled. He had big muscles too. You could see them bulge through his Swamp Land T-shirt.

Mother asked about us joining.

"No problem!" boomed Dinsdale. He smiled at Dilly and me. "Glad to have you aboard! The rest of the gang should be here soon. Say goodbye now ... Your parents can pick you up later."

I was quite happy to stay, especially after Dinsdale told us about all the exciting things we would be doing. Then I noticed Dilly was looking up at Dinsdale with big eyes.

"Well, see you both at supper, Dilly," said Mother. She and Father each gave us a kiss. Then they walked towards the door.

But Dilly ran after them and held on to Mother's skirt.

"I don't want to stay here, Mother," he said, looking over his shoulder at Dinsdale. "I want to go with *you*."

Mother smiled, and said she thought Dilly would have a much better time with The Tiny Tails. Dilly kept shaking his head, so he obviously didn't agree. Then Dinsdale went over.

"I'd just leave him if I were you," he said to Mother in a loud whisper. "He'll be fine once you've gone." Then he turned to Dilly and gave him another big smile. "We'll soon have you shooting down The Big Whizzer, won't we?"

Dilly looked at him with eyes like saucers. Then he opened his mouth …and fired off an ultra-special,150-mile-per-hour super-scream, the kind that makes even large dinosaurs with big muscles go pale green and clap their paws over their ears.

Once Dilly had calmed down, Mother took him to one side and talked to him. But I knew it would do no good. I could see Dilly didn't like Dinsdale, and that he had made his mind up he wasn't going to spend the day with The Tiny Tails.

In the end, Dilly went with Mother

and Father. I stayed with Dinsdale, and had a great time.

Mother and Father's day wasn't so great. When they picked me up later, they looked very tired. Dilly had insisted on going to every playground in Swamp Land. And if that wasn't enough, he hadn't stayed anywhere for longer than two minutes.

Mother and Father didn't get any time to themselves.

So I wasn't surprised when they told Dilly he would have to give The Tiny Tails a try the next day.

Dilly wasn't happy about it, though. As soon as we arrived at The Tiny Tails' office he opened his mouth ... but he never got the chance to scream.

"Hello," said someone in a soft voice. "My name's Dee, and I'll be taking care of The Tiny Tails today."

We looked round, and there was a young lady dinosaur smiling at us. We all smiled back at her ... even Dilly.

It turned out that Dinsdale usually worked in The Big Swamp as a lifeguard. He only looked after The Tiny Tails on Dee's day off. Now she would be in charge for the rest of our stay.

I could tell Dilly liked Dee, mostly because he kept smiling at her. He only stopped smiling when she talked about taking The Tiny Tails to the swamp later.

"Will you make me go down The Big Whizzer?" he said.

"Of course I won't," said Dee. Dilly started smiling again, and slipped his paw into hers.

In fact, within a few days Dilly was going down The Big Whizzer all the time. Mother and Father got their rest, and Dilly and I had so much fun we wanted to stay at Swamp Land forever. Our holiday was over much too soon.

On the way home, Dilly kept talking about Dee. He said he liked her because of the quiet way she spoke to him.

"When Dinsdale talked he made my head ache," he said. "Dee's voice was much nicer."

"Dilly," said Mother. "I do believe you have a crush on Dee."

Dilly turned bright green and we all started laughing – even Dilly!

DILLY AND THE PET NEXT DOOR

"I'm going next door to feed Mr
Darma's rock lizard, Dorla," said Father.
"Would you like to come along?"

Mr Darma is our neighbour. He had
asked us to look after his pet while he
stayed with his daughter for a few days.

I said I would. Father called Dilly, but
he didn't answer. We looked everywhere,
but there was no sign of him.

"I wonder where he can be?" said
Father.

"Why don't we look in the garden?" I
said. Father thought that was a good
idea.

He sounded a little worried, and I
knew why. Father hates it when Dilly
goes missing, even if it's only for a few
minutes. He says we never know what
mischief he'll get up to next.

But the garden was empty, or at least, that's the way it looked at first. Then something very strange happened.

Over by the giant fern, a large clump of swamp reeds started to shake. After a while, a small dinosaur came shuffling backwards out of them. It was Dilly, of course.

"Dilly Dinosaur," said Father. "*What* are you up to?"

Dilly hadn't realised we were there. He jumped when he heard Father's voice, and looked very guilty.

"Er ... nothing, Father," he said. He edged sideways, as if he wanted to hide something from us.

"If I believed that, Dilly," said Father with a sigh, "I'd believe anything. Come on now – out with it."

It didn't take long for Father to find out the truth. Dilly had made himself a

secret hideaway in the bushes. Father
didn't mind that too much. But he did
get cross about something else.

Dilly had taken some things to put in
his hideaway – an old blanket from the
toy cupboard to sit on, a few toys, his
teddy bear ... and some sugared fern
stalks he'd found in the kitchen.

"It's very naughty of you, Dilly," said
Father. "You know you're not supposed
to eat between meals."

"But I needed some food for my game, Father," said Dilly. "I was pretending I'd run away from home."

"I wish you would," I said. Dilly stuck his tongue out at me. I did the same back.

"That's enough, you two," said Father. "You should have asked first, Dilly. Besides, you'd have every stray lizard in the neighbourhood in your hideaway if you left them there. They love sugared fern stalks. Don't do it again … and remember to clean your teeth when we come back."

"Are we going somewhere then, Father?" said Dilly.

"I thought you might like to help us feed Mr Darma's rock lizard," said Father.

"Ooh, yes please!" said Dilly. He started bouncing up and down with excitement.

"But you can only come if you promise to behave," said Father.

"I promise!" said Dilly, and he scampered off towards the back gate.

"Hey, not so fast!" said Father. But Dilly wasn't listening, and we had to chase after him. Father was not pleased.

He should have known Dilly wouldn't wait around if he had a chance to meet somebody's pet. He's crazy about small animals, and he's wanted to see Mr Darma's rock lizard ever since he'd found out Mr Darma had one.

It lived in a cage at the bottom of Mr Darma's garden. I could tell from Dilly's face when he saw it that he liked it a lot. It was bright green, and had big yellow stripes.

"Isn't she beautiful?" said Dilly.

He had his face pressed right up

against the cage. The rock lizard sniffed at him, then licked his snout. Dilly giggled, and said it tickled.

"I think it likes you," said Father, and laughed. "I tell you what ... why don't you feed it while Dorla and I check the house? I told Mr Darma we'd make sure everything was all right."

"Does that mean I can get her out?" said Dilly. He reached out to open the door of the cage.

"No, it certainly does not," said Father quickly. "All you have to do is put some fresh fern leaves through this little gap at the side. I'll fill up the water bottle in a minute. Now, do you think you can manage that?"

"Yes, Father," said Dilly with his I'm-Such-A-Clever-Little-Dinosaur-Look on his face.

I thought Father was taking a big risk. But I didn't say anything.

Father and I walked round the house, checking the doors and windows. We were only gone a little while. Dilly must have thought it would take a lot longer. For when we got back to the garden, we saw that the cage door was open.

Dilly was holding the rock lizard.

"Dilly," shouted Father, running towards him. "What *are* you doing?"

Neither Dilly nor the rock lizard had heard us until that moment. Dilly looked round, surprised ... and the rock lizard leapt out of his arms. Before we could do anything, it ran off into the bushes and disappeared.

Dilly knew he was in trouble.

"It wasn't my fault, Father!" he said after Father had told him off. "He wouldn't have run away if you hadn't shouted."

"That's not the point, is it, Dilly?" said Father. He was very cross. "I didn't get it out of the cage. I only hope for *your* sake that we can find it again. Right ... spread out, you two, and start looking."

We searched Mr Darma's garden for ages, but there was no sign of the rock lizard anywhere. Dilly kept asking me if I thought we'd find him, and I said I didn't know.

"It will probably run out into the street and get run over by a dino-car," I said. Dilly's bottom lip started to quiver. "If we listen carefully we might hear the brakes screeching and then ... SPLAT!"

I was only joking, so I laughed. But Dilly didn't.

He opened his mouth and ... that's right, you guessed it, he let rip with an ultra-special, 150-mile-per-hour super-scream, the kind that makes Father very unhappy.

That's because he'd just seen the rock lizard sitting quietly under a fern leaf. But, of course, by the time Dilly had stopped screaming, it had disappeared again.

We kept searching, but it was no good. Father said we would have to ask everyone in the street to keep an eye out for the rock lizard, and keep our tails crossed that it would turn up.

"I don't know what we'll say to Mr Darma if it doesn't," he said, giving Dilly a stern look.

Dilly didn't say anything.

He was very quiet all through lunch, and he stayed in his room most of the afternoon. Then, at bathtime, I heard Father calling him. But there was no answer.

Dilly had gone missing again.

"Oh no, that's all I need," said Father. "A missing lizard is bad enough, but Dilly going missing twice in one day is more than I can bear. Help me find him, Dorla, will you?"

Dilly wasn't in the house, so we went into the garden. And just as we came out of the back door, that clump of swamp reeds by the giant fern started to shake again. As we watched, Dilly shuffled backwards out of them.

We went over, and saw that he was holding something. It was Mr Darma's rock lizard!

Dilly looked very pleased with himself.

"I remembered what you said about lizards liking sugared fern stalks, Father," he said. "So I put some in my secret hideaway and just waited."

"Well, I'm very impressed, Dilly," said Father with a smile. "Shall we take the rock lizard home now? I'll feel a lot happier once it's back in the cage …"

And that night, at bedtime, I heard Dilly promising Father that he would never, ever be naughty again.

"I'm glad to hear it," said Father.

I didn't listen any more. Sometimes, I thought, parents will believe *anything*.

DILLY DINOSAUR, SUPERSTAR

Rex and the Rockosaurs are signing copies of their new record at the Shopping Cavern. But it's so crowded, Dilly can't get near them. So he lets out one of his ultra-special, 150-mile-per-hour super-screams – and Superstar Rex can hardly believe his ears!

MEET THE WORLD'S NAUGHTIEST DINOSAUR!

Even though, as everyone knows, he's the world's naughtiest dinosaur Dilly still has lots of fans. Now that he is so famous he's started making special visits to bookshops to meet the people who enjoy reading about him. You might be able to meet him in your local bookshop – he usually tries to behave himself!

You can write to this address for more information about Dilly and his books and about other books published by MAMMOTH.

MAMMOTH Press Office,
Michelin House
81 Fulham Road
London SW3 6RB